W9-BVR-619

PALM BEACH COUNTY
LIBRARY SYSTEM
3650 Summit Boulevard
West Palm Beach, FL 33406-4198

Come Sit with Me

Making Friends on the Buddy Bench

BY TINA GALLO

ILLUSTRATED BY LUKE SÉGUIN–MAGEE

Ready-to-Read

SIMON SPOTLIGHT

New York   London   Toronto   Sydney   New Delhi

SIMON SPOTLIGHT
An imprint of Simon & Schuster Children's Publishing Division
1230 Avenue of the Americas, New York, New York 10020
This Simon Spotlight edition August 2019

© 2019 Crayola, Easton, PA 18044-0431. Crayola Oval Logo®, Crayola®, Serpentine Design®,
and Chevron Design® are registered trademarks of Crayola used under license.
Official Licensed Product. All rights reserved, including the right of reproduction
in whole or in part in any form. SIMON SPOTLIGHT, READY-TO-READ, and colophon are
registered trademarks of Simon & Schuster, Inc.

For information about special discounts for bulk purchases, please contact
Simon & Schuster Special Sales at 1-866-506-1949 or business@simonandschuster.com.
Manufactured in the United States of America 0719 LAK
2 4 6 8 10 9 7 5 3 1
ISBN 978-1-5344-5099-8 (hc)
ISBN 978-1-5344-5080-6 (pbk)
ISBN 978-1-5344-5081-3 (eBook)

Today is a big day at school.
We are going to make
a buddy bench!

What is a buddy bench?
If someone is feeling sad or lonely,
they can sit on the bench.

When you see someone
sitting on the bench,
you can ask if they
would like to talk or play.

We are going to paint our bench
so everyone will know it's
a buddy bench.

What color should we paint it?

This is Sophie.

She wants to paint
the buddy bench violet and green.
Those are her best friend Gina's
favorite colors.
Gina moved away last year.
"Every time I see the buddy bench
I will think of Gina and smile,"
Sophie says.

This is Max.
Max wants to paint
the buddy bench
white with red stripes!
"Those are the colors of my
baseball uniform," Max says.

"Playing baseball is my favorite
thing to do.
If the buddy bench
is painted in my team colors,
I'll feel happy every time I see it."

This is Emma.
She thinks the bench
should be yellow!

"Yellow is the color of the sun,
and we should be able to
sit on the buddy bench
and talk about anything
under the sun!" she says.

This is James.
He wants to paint
the buddy bench aquamarine.
Can you guess why?

He loves being at the beach!
"Seeing the color of the ocean
always makes me happy!" he says.

This is Jessica.
Jessica wants to paint the
buddy bench orange.
"My cat is orange," she says.
"I always hug him when I feel sad,
and it makes me feel better!"

There are so many great colors!
We don't know which one to choose.
Which color is the best one
for our buddy bench?

Our teacher has a great idea.
"We don't have to paint
the buddy bench
one color," she says.
"Why don't we use them all?"
We like that idea!

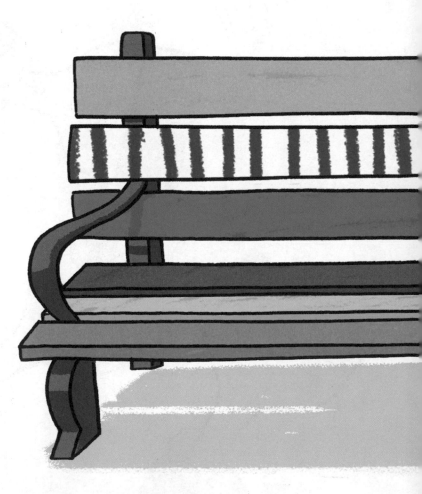

Our teacher smiles.
"I have another idea," she says.
"Let's show that we all had a
hand in painting this very special
buddy bench."

She dips her hand
in her favorite paint color.
She presses her hand
against the bench.
Her handprint is on the buddy bench!
We all do the same thing,
in our special colors.

We love our buddy bench!
We hope kids will remember
to sit on a buddy bench
if they feel sad or lonely.

Everyone needs someone
to talk to once in a while!

A Little History of the Buddy Bench

A few years ago, a boy named Christian thought his family was moving to Germany. He was looking at brochures of possible new schools with his mom. Christian was a little bit nervous. He would be the new kid at school and wouldn't have any friends. He would have no one to play with on the playground on his first day.

But then Christian saw something interesting in a brochure for one of the schools. The school had something called a "buddy bench." If someone was sitting there, the other kids on the playground could ask if he or she wanted to join them.

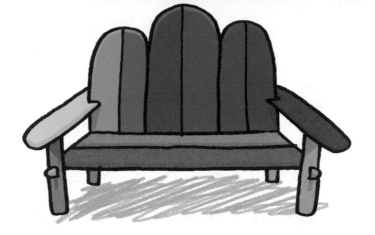

As it turns out, Christian's family did not end up moving to Germany after all. But Christian never forgot the buddy bench. He told his principal at Roundtown Elementary in York, Pennsylvania, about the buddy bench. His principal loved it and had Christian help him pick out a buddy bench for their school.

The buddy bench idea went viral when a national TV program did a story on Christian and his school.

Now there are buddy benches all over the world.

"I didn't like to see kids lonely at recess when everyone is just playing with their friends," Christian said.

These days, there are fewer lonely kids on the playground—and a lot more buddy benches!

Keep in Mind . . . Be Kind!

What if it were you? The easiest way to remember to be kind to others is to think about how you would like to be treated. If you asked someone a question, how would you like them to answer? If something happened to you and you were upset, what would you like your friends to say? Always take a moment to think before you speak to anyone.

Pay attention. Sometimes it's hard for people to talk about their feelings. If one of your friends seems quieter than usual or looks a bit sad, ask if something is wrong. If they say they don't want to talk about it, that's okay, too. But let your friends know you are there for them if they need you.

Being kind is always the way to be. Be kind to everyone you meet—not just your friends or people you know. Kindness is contagious—if you're kind, people will be kind back to you!

Make Your Own Buddy Bench

Talk to your teacher and school principal about adding a buddy bench for your school.

 A good place to put a buddy bench is on the school playground, but it doesn't have to be outdoors. You can put one in the cafeteria or anywhere kids might want a friend to talk to so they don't feel alone.

You can decorate your buddy bench any way you like. You can paint it or put handprints on it like the kids in this story. (Remember to use gloves so your hands don't get paint on them.) You can even paint a saying on it. Maybe there is a friendship quote from a book, poem, or song that you like. Every buddy bench is different, so how yours will look is up to you!

If you don't have room in your school for a buddy bench, you can make a "buddy area" where kids can meet up. Ask your teacher to help.

Remember, if you see someone sitting on a buddy bench, ask them if they would like to talk or hang out. They will probably say, "Come sit with me!" or "Let's play!"